J

Main

Geronimo Stilton

Geronimo Stilton
A learned and brainy
mouse; editor of
The Rodent's Gazette

Thea Stilton
Geronimo's sister and
special correspondent at
The Rodent's Gazette

Trap Stilton
An awful joker;
Geronimo's cousin and
owner of the store
Cheap Junk for Less

Benjamin Stilton
A sweet and loving
nine-year-old mouse;
Geronimo's favorite
nephew

Geronimo Stilton

A CHRISTMAS TALE

Scholastic Inc.

New York   Toronto   London   Auckland   Sydney

Mexico City   New Delhi   Hong Kong   Buenos Aires

ISBN 978-0-439-79131-1

Copyright © 2002 by Edizioni Piemme S.p.A., Via Tiziano 32, 20145 Milan, Italy.

International Rights © Atlantyca S.p.A.

English translation © 2005 by Edizioni Piemme S.p.A.

GERONIMO STILTON names, characters, and related indicia are copyright, trademark, and exclusive license of Atlantyca S.p.A. All rights reserved. The moral right of the author has been asserted.

Based on an original idea by Elisabetta Dami.

www.geronimostilton.com

Published by Scholastic Inc., 557 Broadway, New York, NY 10012. SCHOLASTIC and associated logos are trademarks and/or registered trademarks of Scholastic Inc.

Stilton is the name of a famous English cheese. It is a registered trademark of the Stilton Cheese Makers' Association. For more information, go to www.stiltoncheese.com.

Text by Geronimo Stilton
Original title *Una tenera, tenera, tenera storia sotto la neve*
Cover by Winny Rope
Illustrations by Winny Rope
Graphics by Cheesita de la Pampa

Special thanks to Tracey West
Translated by Lidia Morson Tramontozzi

20 19 18 17 16 15 14 13 12 11   15 16/0

Printed in Malaysia   108
First printing, October 2005

IT WAS A COLD DECEMBER MORNING

How cold was it, you ask? It was so cold that the cheese sandwich I had for breakfast turned into a **CHEESE POPSICLE**!

I zipped up my winter coat. I wrapped my favorite scarf around my neck. It's cheddar yellow. My favorite nephew, Benjamin, gave it to me. It always keeps my snout very warm! Then I stepped out of my mouse hole* into the **frozen air**.

I scampered down the street, toward the center of town. I had just taken a few steps when it began to snow! Snowflakes

* I live at 8 Mouseford Lane. By the way, my name is Stilton, Geronimo Stilton. I am the publisher and editor of *The Rodent's Gazette*, the most famous newspaper on Mouse Island!

Big mice, small mice,
tall rats, short rats...
they were all busy
Christmas shopping!

swirled down from the sky. They landed on my whiskers like tiny WHITE BUTTERFLIES.

I smiled. It was snowing on Christmas Eve! How perfect! As I walked past the shops, I began to hum that famous Christmas carol *"Silent Mice."*

All of New Mouse City seemed to be in the *Christmas spirit*. Bright lights

A mouse rushed down the street. **WHAM!** Our heads crashed with a crunch.

flickered in the store windows. Mice scurried by, their arms filled with presents.

I gazed up at the star on top of a Christmas tree when suddenly...

WHAM! I crashed into a mouse crossing the street! He carried an enormouse red box. He seemed to be in quite a rush.

SLAM! I slipped on the ice. I landed right on top of my poor tail. Ouch!

I stood up, rubbing my tail. A look of

I slipped on the ice... ...and landed on my poor tail!

surprise came across the mouse's face. "*Geronimo Stilton*! Is that you?"

I couldn't believe it. It was my old friend from school, **Buddy Pawpal**.

"Buddy! What are you doing here?" I asked.

"Shopping, of course," Buddy said. "I want to *impress* my friends and relatives, so I'm buying all of the HOTTEST gifts. Have you seen the new Cheese-o-Matic? It slices, dices, grates, grinds, chops, mashes, smashes—and then it washes itself when it's done! It costs a **fortune**, but it's worth it."

"Uh, no, I haven't heard of it," I replied.

"Have you bought your gifts yet?" Buddy asked. "I bet you spent a lot of **money**, right?"

"I don't think how much money you

spend on a gift is important," I said. "It's the *thought* that counts."

Buddy laughed and slapped me on the back. "Oh, Geronimo, you always were a STRaNge MouSe!" he said. Then he hurried away, calling out behind him. *"Merry Christmas! Happy New Year! Season's Greetings! Happy Holidays!"*

Dear Stilton... ...my old friend. Merry Christmas! Happy New Year! Season's Greetings! Happy Holidays! Good tidings to you!

Buy! Buy! Buy!

I spent the morning walking in the snow and looking at the decorations all around New Mouse City. It was lunchtime when I got back home. All that walking had made me **HUNGRY!** I chomped on a triple-decker cheese sandwich.

I yawned. All that walking had made me tired, too! But it was Christmas Eve, and I was expecting a houseful of guests. I decided

to take a nap so I would be well rested in the evening.

First I took a warm bath with **BLUe CHeese-sCenteD** bubbles. Then I put on my soft pajamas decorated with pepperoni pizza slices. Finally, I fed **HANNIBAL**, my little red fish.

"Have some crumbs of Christmas pie, *my friend!*" I said.

I snuggled into my comfy couch. Outside, the **snow** was really coming down. I felt *warm and cozy.* I turned on the TV.

A loud commercial blared out.

"BUY! BUY! BUY! HURRY BEFORE IT'S TOO LATE!"

I clicked off the TV and turned on the radio instead. But it wasn't any better. A horrible jingle filled my ears.

"**Shop! Shop! Shop!**
Shop until you drop!
If you don't spend your money
Your friends will look at you funny!"

I shut off the radio and picked up a magazine. But every page had an ad for a new product. Uncle Ratsy's Whisker Polish! Chester's Cheddar Soda Pop! *RATZOIDS, THE HOTTEST VIDEO GAME OF THE YEAR*!

I closed the magazine. Then I closed my eyes and started to nap. But before I could

fall asleep, the phone **rang**.

"This is Stilton, *Geronimo Stilton*," I answered.

"**Mr. Stilton, I can tell you are a smart mouse,**" said the squeaky voice on the other end. "**That is why I know you will take me up on this special offer. For just $19.99 you can own your very own ANTICAT ALARM!**"

"But there aren't any **CATS** in New Mouse City!" I said.

"**But what if there were? Then you'd be in big trouble without this alarm, wouldn't you? So you'd better buy it, Mr. Stilton!**"

I couldn't take it anymore. "**LEAVE ME ALONE!**" I cried. Then I slammed down the receiver.

I *snuggled* back into the couch. Then I looked out the window at the falling snow.

Even that was ruined!

A plane flew across the sky. It dragged a sign behind it...

SHOP TODAY AT SQUEAKY STEVE'S!
HURRY UP! IT'S CHRISTMAS EVE!

The telephone rang again.

I grabbed the phone. "STOP CALLING ME! I DON'T WANT TO BUY ANYTHING! LEAVE ME ALooooooooONE!"

On the other end, a tiny voice squeaked in surprise.

"Uncle Geronimo! Are you all right?"

I Don't Want to Be Alone!

It was my nephew Benjamin. **1**
I cheered up right away. **I love Benjamin**! He is the sweetest little mouselet in the whole world.

"I'm all right, Benjamin," I answered. "I can't wait to see you tonight for Christmas Eve."

"But that's why I'm calling," Benjamin said. "I wanted to wish you a *Merry Christmas* before I leave with Aunt Thea." **2**

I could not believe my ears. "Leaving?" I asked. "Aren't you going to spend Christmas here with me, like you do every year?"

I heard my sister's voice next.

"We are going on a cruise to a tropical island. I am not inviting you because you always get SEASICK! See ya, big brother."

I hung up the phone and frowned. Yes, I do get SEASICK. But I couldn't believe my sister would leave me on *Christmas!* And to take Benjamin with her, too! It was downright cruel.

I called my cousin Trap ③ next to make sure he was still coming. He told me he was going to San Mouscisco to take a cooking class.

I sighed. "It sounds like fun, Trap," I said. "Have a nice trip."

Was I really going to be alone on Christmas? I called the rest of my family to see what they were doing.

My grandfather William Shortpaws
(4) was packing up his cheese-
colored camper. He was going on a
cheese-tasting tour in Cheddarton
with his cook, Tina Spicytail (5).

My dear aunt Sweetfur (6) was going
to a concert in Mouseport. I understood.
She adores the great *classical* composer
Mousart.

I called every relative I could think of—
even Uncle Samuel S. Stingysnout (7)! He
never says no to a free meal. But even he
said he was busy!

I tried not to PANIC. My family
was away. But I still had my friends,
didn't I?

I did not. I called all of my friends from
The Rodent's Gazette, but they were all busy.
Pinky Pick (8), my assistant editor, was going

to a **FUZZY FUZZBORN** concert. Kreamy
O'Cheddar ⑨, my right-hand mouse, was
going **skiing** on Slipperyslopes Glacier.
Mousella MacMouser ⑩, Merenguita
Gingermouse ⑪, Zeppola Zap ⑫, Blasco
Tabasco ⑬, and Larry Keys ⑭ were going
to an **art show** in Mousefort Beach.

You will not believe who I called next.
I phoned Creepella von Cacklefur ⑮, the
spooky rodent who wants to marry me. But
she was going to visit her creepy family in
the **VALLEY OF THE VAIN VAMPIRES**.

So it was true. I was going to spend

Christmas all alone! I was so sad that I began to cry. Salty tears **soaked** my whiskers.

"I don't want to be alone!" I wailed. "What kind of Christmas will I have without my friends and family?"

I hugged Hannibal's fishbowl.

"You are the only one who loves me, Hannibal!" I sobbed.

Hannibal, the little red fish

IT WOULD HAVE BEEN SUCH A NICE CHRISTMAS...

I looked around my apartment. Tiny paper hearts decorated the tree. The table was set with place cards. Everything looked so **beautiful**! But it only made me sadder. My friends and family would have liked the decorations so much! But now they would never see them.

I looked at the gifts under the tree. I had made them with my own paws! A **paperweight** for Grandfather

William. A **photo frame** for Aunt Sweetfur. **Chocolate sweets** for Trap. **Sweet-smelling sachets** for Thea. And for Benjamin, a **letter** that told him how much I loved him.

Thinking of Benjamin made me sad again. I looked at the table where I had set up our Christmas game, **Mouse-o-mania**. I love Hannibal, but I can't play board games with him. If only my friends and family were coming . . .

"We would have had so much fun," I said, drying my tears. *"It would have been such a nice Christmas!"*

It's fun to play **Mouse-o-mania** on Christmas!

Everything was ready for my friends...
It would have been such a nice Christmas!

Geronimo

Thea

Grandfather
William

Tina
Spicytail

Benjamin

Uncle
Stingysnout

Trap

Aunt
Sweetfur

STILTOD?
GERODIBO STILTOD?

I could not bear to look at the presents and decorations. I put on my winter coat again and went outside. Heavy snow fell from the sky. It reminded me of Parmesan flakes shaking down on *pasta*.

I had not gone far when I bumped into a figure wrapped in scarves. THIN SCARVES, LONG SCARVES, **WIDE SCARVES**, **HEAVY SCARVES**, you name it — this rodent looked like a scarf mummy!

"Stiltod? Gerodibo Stiltod?" the strange figure mumbled.

Then I knew who it was — Mrs. Ratillis, the sweet old lady who lives in the apartment above mine. I could tell by the way she

talked that she had a **bad cold**.

"Mrs. Ratillis, you should be inside on a day like this!" I said. "Let me take you home."

I love Mrs. Ratillis. Before I go to work, I always bring her a hunk of cheese. And I make sure she gets a free copy of *The Rodent's Gazette*. It's in large print because she has poor eyesight.

Mrs. Ratillis began to sob under her scarves. "Dear Gerodibo, I dan't find Doonflower!"

It was hard to understand Mrs. Ratillis through her stuffy snout. But I knew what she meant.

"You can't find Moonflower, your nightingale?" I asked.

She nodded. "My poor Doonflower flew out the window.

Mrs. Ratillis

Moonflower

Where could he be? What a sad dight I will hab all by myself!"

"You will not be alone tonight, Mrs. Ratillis," I said quickly. "Come to my place at seven. *We will have a wonderful Christmas together!*"

I told Mrs. Ratillis that I would look for Moonflower. I took her up to her apartment. Then I went back out.

It was so cold! I began to wish I had borrowed some scarves from Mrs. Ratillis. Soon **icicles** hung from my whiskers. I hate when that happens!

But I had made a promise to Mrs. Ratillis. I walked up and down the streets of New Mouse City, looking for her bird.

"Moooooooooonflower!"

But I could not find the nightingale anywhere!

RATTINA'S DREAM
COMES TRUE

I kept walking. The snow kept falling. It was very cold. I hummed a Christmas tune to keep warm: "*Rudolph the Red-Nosed Rodent*." But it didn't help. Soon I felt an **icicle** hanging from my snout.

I hate when that happens!

I walked past the biggest toy store in the city. That is when I noticed a woman holding the paw of a tiny blond mouse. They were both staring at the store window.

"Look, Mommy," the little girl said. "That is the **teddy bear** I always dreamed of!"

Curious, I stepped closer to the window. A sweet-looking **stuffed bear** sat on a pillow in the store display. Around its neck

It was the teddy bear of her dreams. . . .

was a big yellow bow the color of smooth American cheese.

I got a warm feeling inside. It was a feeling so **warm** that it melted the icicle on my snout!

I quickly ran into the store. The salesmouse recognized me right away.

"Mr. Stilton! How may I help you?"

"I'd like to buy that **teddy bear** in the window, please," I said.

Minutes later, I rushed out of the store. I walked up to the mommy mouse and her daughter. I took off my cap and bowed.

"May I introduce myself?" I asked. "My name is Stilton, *Geronimo Stilton*."

The mommy mouse turned red. "*Geronimo Stilton*? The famouse newspaper mouse?" she said. "It is an honor to meet you."

I looked at the little **mouselet**. "I would

like to give this **teddy bear** to your daughter as a gift," I said. "Would that be all right?"

The woman's eyes got teary. "That is **too much!**" she said.

I smiled. "It is not **too much** if it will make your daughter's dream come true."

I gave the teddy bear to the cute little mouselet.

"You are so kind, Mr. Stilton," said the woman. "Rattina, thank Mr. Stilton."

Rattina squeaked with delight and hugged the **stuffed bear**. "Thank you, thank you, thank you!" she cried. Then she turned to her mother. "Are we going home?"

Her mother sighed. "There is no hurry. We're all alone. No one is waiting for us there."

I had an idea.

"Allow me to invite you to my home for Christmas," I said. "Come to 8 Mouseford Lane at seven o'clock. I will make a meal that is whisker-licking good. *We will have a wonderful Christmas together!*"

I bowed . . .

GIVE ME YOUR MONEY!

I decided to head back home. The snow was almost up to my knees! I could feel an **icicle** hanging from each of my ears.

I hate when that happens!

I took a shortcut through the park.

"Moooooonflower!" I called out.

Suddenly, I heard a yell behind me.

"HEY YOU! STOP RIGHT THERE!"

I turned and saw a dark shadow.

"Give me your money!" the mysterious rodent shouted.

Normally, I would have been **afraid**. But it was Christmas Eve. I wanted to help this mouse.

"Don't you know it's Christmas Eve?" I said softly.

"Give me your money!" the mouse said again. But this time, his voice was

shaking. Then I heard him sob.

I walked up to him. "Are you all right? May I help you?" I asked.

Now I could see the mouse in the light of the streetlamp. He was **SHORT** and **SKINNY** with a sad look in his eyes.

"I am so sorry," he said in a soft voice. "I've never done this before. But I didn't know what else to do. If I told you, you'd understand, I promise. But you don't want to listen to me, I'm sure."

I put my paw on his shoulder. "I would be happy to listen to you," I said. "Come to my house tonight. *We can talk over a slice of nice ripe cheese.*"

Then another voice rang through the night. "What is going on here?" a police mouse asked us.

"Everything is fine, Officer," I said.

The police mouse glanced at the SKINNY mouse by my side. He frowned. "Hmmm. And who is this?"

"He is a friend," I said. "We were about to go to my house for *Christmas Eve* supper."

The police mouse sighed. "Lucky you," he said. "My shift is almost over. But I'm all alone tonight."

"Then come with us!" I said. "I'll see both of you at seven o'clock at 8 Mouseford Lane. Ring the buzzer for STILTON. *We will have a wonderful Christmas together!*"

EVERY JOB
IS IMPORTANT

I decided to look in one more place for Moonflower. I headed to the harbor. It was very cold by the water. Soon I could feel an **icicle** hanging from the tip of my tail.

I hate when that happens!

"Mooooonflower!" I called out. "**Mooooonflower!**"

"Hey, Mister!" a small voice cried. It surprised me! I slipped on a fish bone.

Splat! I landed inside a **BARREL** of rotten fish. I climbed out of the slippery barrel. **Sardine bones** stuck to my fur. A stinky lobster sat on top of my head. I brushed off the **slimy mess**. Then I saw a very tiny mouse standing in front of me.

"Sir, can you help me?" he squeaked. "My name is **Speck**. I was looking for my daddy, but I got lost."

I smiled. "Of course I'll help you. Where are your dad and mom?"

"I don't have a mom anymore," the little mouse said. "Daddy works at a restaurant here at the harbor. He has a very IMPORTANT job!"

I took his little paw in mine. The harbor was lined with seafood restaurants. We checked them out, one by one. But Speck did not see his father in any of them.

Then we came to a VERY EXPENSIVE-LOOKING RESTAURANT. The host walked up to us. My fur and coat were still dripping with **fish guts**. The host frowned and held his nose.

"WHO ARE YOU? WHAT DO YOU WANT?" he asked sharply.

"My name is Stilton, *Geronimo Stilton*," I said. "This little mouse is lost. He is looking for his father. Does he work here?"

The mouse snorted. "If you are *Geronimo Stilton*, then I am **SANTA MOUSE**!" he said. "*Stilton* is a **BIG CHEESE** in this town. He is not a **smelly sewer rat** like you. Get out of here!"

I started to protest. But then Speck ran toward the restaurant's kitchen.

"Daddy! Daddy!" he cried.

A rodent wearing a cook's apron came out. He hugged the little mouse.

"Is everything OK, Speck?" he asked.

The snooty host sniffed. "This is a restaurant, not a day-care center!" he said. He glared at the cook. "You are fired! That will teach you to waste time instead of working."

Then one of the waiters ran over to the host. The waiter pointed at me and whispered something in the host's ear. The host turned as pale as a piece of MOZZARELLA.

"Are you sure?" he asked the waiter.

The waiter nodded. I saw **drops of sweat** form on the host's whiskers.

"Mr. *Stilton*, I had no idea it was really you," he said. "Please, allow me to serve you dinner, Mr. *Stilton*. We would be **proud** to serve such a **famouse rodent** as yourself, Mr. *Stilton*."

"I WILL NOT STAY HERE ANOTHER SECOND!" I said angrily. I turned to **Speck's** father. "Come with me. I will help you get another job where you will be treated with more **respect**!"

We left with our HEADS HELD HIGH.

Speck looked up at me as we walked down the street. "Daddy is a cook. That is a very IMPORTANT job, isn't it?"

"Of course it is," I replied. "Every job is important. It takes all kinds of mice to make the world go round. And what job could be more IMPORTANT than feeding hungry mice?"

Then I shook his father's paw. "Come to my home at 8 Mouseford Lane at seven o'clock tonight. *We will have a wonderful Christmas together!*"

I hurried home. My heart felt as light as a *cheese puff*. I was not going to be alone on Christmas!

Still, I had to find Moonflower. I called out the nightingale's name all the way home. But I didn't see him anywhere.

I reached the front of my building, feeling

sad. What was I going to tell Mrs. Ratillis?

Then a heard a little **chirp**. It was coming from the mailbox. There, trembling from the cold, was Moonflower! I bundled

chirp!

chirp!

chirp!

him under my jacket and ran upstairs to find Mrs. Ratillis.

"**DOONFLOWER**!" she cried out.

I left them both and walked downstairs

to my apartment. I reached for the doorknob...

But the door was open!

I carefully stepped inside.

It was **dark**. Not a single light was on.

What was going on?

WHY WERE ALL THE LIGHTS OFF?

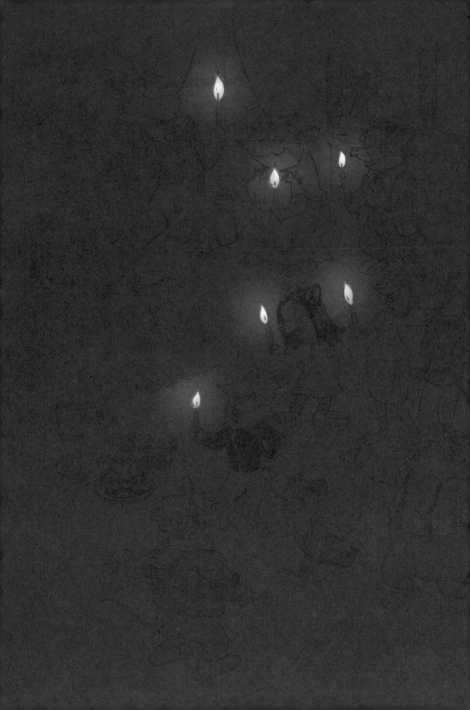

A Wonderful Christmas Together

The lights suddenly came on. All of my **friends and family** were there! They began to sing:

Outside it is snowing

But inside we are glowing

Christmas is here

And what we hold dear

Is the gift we can't get enough of

The greatest gift of all . . .

the gift of Love!

I was shocked. "But I thought you were all going away!" I said.

"Of course not," Thea said. "We just wanted to **surprise** you. Christmas wouldn't be Christmas without you, Gerrykins!"

"We love spending the holiday with all our family and friends," said Aunt Sweetfur.

"And it's **FREE**!" added Uncle Samuel Stingyfur.

Benjamin ran up and hugged me. "**I love you**, Uncle Geronimo. This is going to be the best Christmas ever!"

Soon all of the new friends I had met that day arrived. We all sat around the table. Trap stood up and clinked a glass with his spoon. "**SPEECH! SPEECH!**" he cried.

I cleared my throat. "My whiskers are fluttering with happiness," I began. "It is

wonderful to be with all of my loved ones this year. And now I have many new friends, too! I am a very **lucky** mouse."

I wiped a tear from my eye.

Trap rubbed his tummy. **"THAT'S VERY MOVING, GERONIMO. NOW LET'S EAT!"** he shouted.

I ran into the kitchen. I came back carrying a Christmas feast. I had made a Swiss cheese pie, a big salad with **BLUE CHEESE CHUNKS**, cheddar cheese soup, and **A SMALL CHRISTMAS TREE MADE OF CREAM CHEESE!** Everyone licked their whiskers.

"HURRAY FOR GERONIMO!" they cheered.

I smiled. It was exactly how I dreamed my Christmas would be!

After dinner, Benjamin and I cleared the table. I looked out the window. The **snow** had stopped falling, and the sky was clear.

Against the black sky, I saw a very tiny, very bright star. It fell through the sky.

"Look, Benjamin. A falling star," I whispered. "Let's make a wish."

I held Benjamin's paw, and we watched until the star disappeared. I don't know for sure what Benjamin wished for. But I bet he had the same wish as I did: to be able to spend many, many, many more Christmases like this one. *Together!*

ALL WE NEED IS LOVE

Dear mouse friends, how will you spend your Christmas? I hope you will spend it with someone who loves you.

That is something I learned a long time ago. You can have all the **cheese** in the world, but if you don't have love in your life, the cheese will taste like **moldy socks**! *Love* makes everything better.

Look around. There is *Love* all around you — with your family, your friends, even your pets. Imagine if everyone spread this *Love* all around the world.

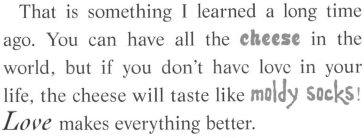

Then it would be Christmas every day!

Geronimo Stilton